TE DEUM

Kristina Howells

To Lisa
All the best
Kristina Howells

MINERVA PRESS
LONDON
MIAMI   RIO DE JANEIRO   DELHI

TE DEUM
Copyright © Kristina Howells 2001

All Rights Reserved

No part of this book may be reproduced in any form
by photocopying or by any electronic or mechanical means,
including information storage or retrieval systems,
without permission in writing from both the copyright
owner and the publisher of this book.

ISBN 0 75411 524 0

First Published 2001 by
MINERVA PRESS
315–317 Regent Street
London W1R 7YB

Printed in Great Britain for Minerva Press

TE DEUM

Chapter One

It was one party that Kate wished she had never attended. Jane, her best friend of seven years, was holding her twenty-fifth birthday bash at an exclusive wine bar in London.

'Kate, you better not let me down,' exclaimed Jane over the phone to Kate.

'No Jane, I won't,' replied Kate.

'I'll see you at seven o'clock in Henry's on Saturday, and we'll go on from there.'

'All right, sweetie, see you then.'

Kate was usually excited about birthdays, especially as every time Jane and herself went out they always managed to have fun. Kate met Jane whilst they were studying for their degrees at music college in 1991. Jane, a flautist, and Kate, an up-and-coming composer, hadn't seen each other in four months. Kate had just had her new work *Te Deum* premiered in New York and in Paris. She had started to make a name for herself and Jane was proud of her best friend.

Jane couldn't wait to see her, and tell her all about her engagement to Darren, as well as catching up with life in general. Deep down she knew Kate wouldn't be happy about the engagement, so she decided to get Darren to invite some of his friends from the gym where he worked out.

'Maybe that will cheer her up,' murmured Jane.

'She has to accept that you cannot remain single for ever,' said Darren. 'It will be hard for her at first, considering that she's an up-and-coming prolific composer.

'I know,' replied Jane.

'So I'll only introduce her to my finest friends.'

'Knowing Kate, Darren, she's rather choosy about who she is seen with, because she finds it hard to trust anyone. Especially non-musicians and artists in general.'

'All right, we will just have to see how things go for her. But

Jane darling, don't worry, she'll have a great time. Trust me!'

Soon it was Jane's birthday. Jane and Darren were excited about announcing their engagement, and Jane couldn't wait to catch up with Kate. Four months seemed a lifetime for them both. So much had happened and Jane was looking forward to revealing it all.

Seven o'clock had now arrived. Kate walked in looking absolutely stunning. Jane was impressed by the way she looked. Kate wore a emerald evening gown that she bought in New York. It matched her green eyes and her long blonde hair.

'Oh my, Kate, you look wonderful.'

'Thank you, Jane. Happy birthday, and here's a little something from New York for you.'

'Thank you, Kate.'

Jane, opening up the box, liked the gift Kate bought her – a little statue of a woman playing the flute and a treble clef hair clip which Jane could use to put up her long blonde hair, when she played the flute in concerts.

'Well, Jane, how have things been for you, are you still playing in the London Contemporary Orchestra?'

'Yes but I didn't get the principal flute audition, as I was not at my best on the day, so I have to stick with playing second flute for the time being.'

'I'm sorry to hear that; well, what else has happened since I last saw you?'

'Not a lot Kate, except… Do you remember I was telling you all about my last boyfriend Darren?'

'I think so, wasn't he the one you met when I was last in London, who works in the City?'

'Yes, well, Kate, I have something to tell you about Darren and me.'

'What's that? No, don't tell me, you're pregnant and expecting his baby!'

'No, Kate, it's nothing like that! He's asked me to marry him and I said yes.'

'Congratulations! Where is he?'

'He's over there!'

Jane and Kate began to walk over towards the bar where

Darren was standing with his friends.

'Kate, do you remember Darren?'

'Yes, I do. Hello Darren.'

'Hello Kate, what would you like to drink?'

'Oh, just a glass of red wine. Thank you. I believe congratulations are in order – so have you set a date yet?'

'No Kate, but when we do, you'll be the first to know.'

Kate soon started to feel out of place. On the surface she was happy that Jane was to be married. Yet, deep down she wished it could be how it was four months ago.

Kate continued making polite conversation – even to Darren's friends. But she found it all rather boring.

As Kate followed the others to the arranged party bash at the exclusive wine bar, close to Henry's in Piccadilly, she caught a glimpse of a man looking out of the window in the bar. Ignoring him, she went to sit down with a large glass of red wine and waited for one of Darren's friends to entertain her further.

'I must go to the ladies,' said Kate eagerly, and got up from her seat and went over to the man who'd caught her eye as she walked in. Kate found the young man very handsome, he had dark hair, slim and very trendily dressed.

'Excuse me, are you waiting for someone?'

'No,' he replied.

'Would you care to join my friends and me in a little birthday celebration and an engagement?'

'I would love too. Would you like a drink?'

'Um, a large glass of red wine, please.'

'I'll bring it straight over.'

When Kate went back to sit down, she found Jane telling her all about her future plans, and warning her to be careful about the guy she had just pulled. Kate, not listening to Jane's advice, suggested to her that she would join the others at Club 81 later.

Kate couldn't believe her luck, especially as the guy she had just met was a doctor. The only doctors she ever came across were in a surgery or in hospitals when visiting friends, she didn't think they had a social life as well. His name was Leon.

Leon seemed to be a very nice person. He also had the natural ability to make Kate feel at ease.

'If we are going to make that nightclub, I need to get some money out of the cash machine,' hinted Leon in his deep confusing Irish/American accent.

'All right,' replied Kate.

Unfortunately Leon couldn't remember his pin number and because of it, he lost his bank card in the machine.

'Oh what an idiot!' he cried. 'I'm sorry Kate.'

'Oh well, not to worry. I'm too tired to go clubbing anyway.'

'Listen, Kate, how would you like to come back to my flat in Chelsea for chicken, boiled potatoes and a salad to make up for it. Along with a bottle of wine to wash it all down with.'

'That sounds lovely, why not!'

Leon and Kate began to walk down towards Trafalgar Square to catch a cab back to his place in Chelsea. It seemed to have taken the cab driver no time at all to get there. Leon shared the flat with Tom, an architect.

'Please do make yourself feel comfortable, while I get supper prepared,' said Leon as they walked through the door.

Kate began to walk into the living room. On the way she marvelled at the photography displayed on the walls in the hallway. She had never seen pictures of animals like these, except on television or in magazines.

'Did you go to Africa and take these pictures on the wall?'

'No, but my landlord Tom did.'

'He's really good.'

'Anyway supper will be ready soon,' interrupted Leon rather sharply.

Kate didn't take any notice of the sharp edge in his voice, as she concentrated on the pictures.

Over dinner they managed to engage themselves with further polite conversation. Kate started to talk openly about the first time she went to Paris as a composer, and how it felt to have a piece of music which she wrote premier in one of the world's most cultural cities.

Kate hadn't always dreamt of being a composer. It first started off as a hobby, as she really wanted to be an opera singer – that's what she originally trained in. Kate would have made it, if it hadn't been for this horrible man who exploited her, and who almost tried to kill her when he threatened her with a knife.

It had taken Kate five years to pick herself up, and get over this man who ruined her career as a singer. Determined not to allow this to happen again, Kate was very careful about whom she chose to go out with. Deep down Kate was longing to be in love, and to be loved by one man whom she could trust. Yet there was this hidden fear that prevented her from taking the next step in a relationship. So throwing herself into her work as a composer seemed the only answer to healing the inner pain of longing and romance, as well as her retaining her sanity and inner peace.

When Leon began to speak of his past, Kate didn't know what to make of it all or him. She liked him a lot and felt a yearning for him. When Leon spoke of some aspects of his work, Kate couldn't help but laugh. Leon wasn't offended, he liked her sense of humour, and felt very attracted to her.

'Well I'm tired,' said Kate.

'You can always stay and share my bed. I promise I won't do anything you don't want to do.'

'Okay.'

As they got into bed, Kate and Leon began to kiss and cuddle the night away. Kate felt comfortable lying in his arms. The warmth from his body made her feel secure. This was something she hadn't experienced in months, the idea of being close to someone; and feeling this gently sent her to sleep.

Chapter Two

The next day Kate woke up thinking how comforting it was to be in a man's arms again when Tom knocked loudly on the door and shouted, 'Come on, Leon, open the door, tea's up.'

'Okay, mate, I'm coming,' replied Leon. 'I'm sorry, Kate, but I'm afraid I have to go to work in an hour, and I left a note asking Tom to wake us up.'

'Oh well, I have a lot to get done today anyway. But will I get to see you again?'

'Look, here is my number; give me a call and we will sort something out.'

'All right.'

Kate drank the tea that Tom made and quickly made her way back to her parents' house in Orpington, Kent.

'Have a fun day at work, Leon, and I'll call you later.'

'See you, Kate.'

'Yeah, see you.'

She then lent over Leon and kissed him lightly on the lips before heading towards Fulham Broadway tube station.

While Kate was on the train going back home, she started to feel different and as a result, all sorts of thoughts were going through her mind. The uncertainty of what Leon was about was plaguing her. It all seemed too good to be true.

What if he was making all of it up? The fact that he was a doctor, and that he treated Mel Gibson in a Californian hospital! But if he was lying what kind of man was he? thought Kate.

For the moment, Kate was happy just to be his friend, especially as the deadline for her new work *Sanctus Christe* didn't have to be with EMI records until the end of June – which gave her plenty of time to get to know him.

It didn't take Kate all that long to get home. She left Leon at eight o'clock and was home by ten. All Kate could do was think about Leon, even when she was continuing her work on *Sanctus*

Christe. In the end she decided to give him a call. There was no answer so she left a message on his answer machine.

Then at ten o'clock that Sunday night, Leon called her back. They decided to set a date for the following Friday at nine thirty at the same place where they'd first met.

Kate couldn't wait to see him again. She hoped the week would end quickly. But it didn't.

During the week Kate was having difficulties sleeping and even eating – she was just too excited. However, when Friday finally arrived, she began to have her doubts.

On the way to London, Kate bumped into an old friend from her college days. She hadn't seen Clive in ages. The last time they had met was at a concert two years previously. Jane was playing the flute and Clive the trumpet. They were playing *Petrushka* by Stravinsky with the London Philharmonic Orchestra.

Kate had been impressed by that performance, and from then on she was inspired by Stravinsky – the way he made use of the rhythmical phrases and use of dissonances had always affected her. These were the many musical devices she used in her first work, *Te Deum.*

Kate was attracted to Clive. She always thought of him as handsome and she wished he was available. Especially as he was the only one who seemed to understand her.

Clive accepted Kate's offer of a drink at the wine bar where she was to meet Leon later. At least if Leon didn't turn up, she wouldn't look a fool on her own.

Nine thirty soon arrived. There was no sign of Leon. Kate began to feel a little agitated but was glad of Clive's company.

'As soon as Leon walks in, I'll have to go, Kate.'

'All right, it was nice to see you again, Clive.'

'You too, Kate. Look, here is my number and my address, if you want to keep in touch.'

'Thanks, Clive.'

Then at that point Leon walked in, and Clive said his goodbyes and left.

'Hello, Kate. Sorry I'm late.'

'No worries, but you could get me a large glass of red wine to make up for it.'

'Okay.'

When Leon got back from the bar they continued their conversation. Kate was fascinated with what he had to say. He appeared on the surface to be a man of mystery – a lot of what he said didn't seem to add up. It seemed that his lifetime experiences were a jigsaw puzzle that just didn't seem to fit.

After several hours in the wine bar, Kate and Leon grabbed a cab back to his place in Chelsea. When they arrived Tom was at home entertaining some friends.

'Hello, Kate,' said Tom. 'Come and sit down.'

'Hello, Tom,' replied Kate.

'What would you like to drink, Kate?' asked Leon.

'A glass of wine, please.'

As Leon went into the kitchen to get a bottle of wine for Kate and himself to share, Tom began to introduce Kate to his friends. Kate commented on Tom's photographs in the hall.

'They are the best I have seen,' commented Kate.

Tom's friends were really business associates from work. But every so often he entertained them at his home. Kate found them quite humorous. She'd always thought that men and women who worked in the City were boring and dull with very little passion about anything except their work. She had always found them stuck up, obstinate and downright rude.

But these guys certainly were not that. They made Kate feel welcome, which Leon didn't seem very much at ease with. It was as if he was jealous of Tom's friends, and of Tom who had made her feel welcome, and accepted her as an acquaintance.

When Tom's friends finally left and Tom went to bed, Kate and Leon began to embrace and kiss on the sofa.

Leon had the week off from work and asked Kate to stay with him. Kate happily agreed. She couldn't believe that this man who she had only just met wanted to spend a whole week with her.

After some time on the sofa, Leon took Kate by the hand and led her to the bedroom. The bedroom was very small. There were lots of boxes everywhere and the room was very untidy. It looked like an atom bomb had hit it.

Leon started slowly to undress Kate, bit by bit, and Kate did the same. Soon they were both naked, kissing and cuddling on the

12

bed.

Leon reached over to the bedside cabinet and opened the drawer to get a condom. Kate, in the heat of passion, helped to put it on whilst Leon was kissing her body.

As they started to make love, Kate felt for the first time whole. It was if he was the missing piece in a jigsaw puzzle. He felt good. Leon was the first man ever to touch her inner soul whilst making love. And this she didn't want to stop.

It didn't take Leon long to climax. Afterwards, Leon gave her a thank you kiss and they both fell asleep in each others' arms, still reeling from the passion that they had experienced together for the first time in their relationship.

Chapter Three

Leon and Kate stayed in bed till 2 p.m. Kate never usually stayed in bed that long. Leon got up first to run Kate a bath, as well as to cook her a fry-up.

'Bath's ready,' shouted Leon.

'Thanks.'

While Kate was in the bath, Leon began to make a few phone calls. One was to his good friend Niva. Niva originally came from Saudi Arabia and moved to Britain with her family when she was two years old.

Niva worked for a top international bank in the City as a finance manager. Leon and Niva used to live with each other for ten years without her parents' knowledge. Niva's dad would have disowned her if he had ever found out.

Then on VE day in Hyde Park, Niva's dad caught them together and Niva finished with Leon. However, they still remained as close as they were when they lived together. Leon asked Niva a number of times for her hand in marriage. He was besotted with her.

But unknown to Kate, Leon was still in love with her. Niva paid his rent, and helped him get work. Only because when Leon gets a job, he prefers to spend his days in bed nursing a hangover so that he can continue lying and drinking.

'Breakfast is ready, Kate.'

'I'm coming.'

Kate began to get dress quickly, and made her way to the living room where breakfast was waiting for her.

'I hope it's all right, Kate.'

'It looks fine, Leon.'

'Listen Kate, whilst you were in the bath I had a phone call asking me to go to America on Monday, and I shall be there for a week.'

'Why, Leon?' quizzed Kate.

14

'I'd rather not say. Anyway, I'm not going until Monday and today's only Saturday.'

'Okay, so what are we going to do today?' asked Kate, changing the subject rather quickly, 'as it looks lovely and sunny outside.'

'We can go down to Tower Hill, and walk along the river, if you want?'

'That sounds cool.'

After Kate had eaten her breakfast, and Leon had washed up, they began to walk towards Fulham Broadway tube station.

Kate had not been to this area of London for quite a while. She used to come down to Tower Bridge quite a lot when she was studying at the Guildhall School of Music and Drama. She found it peaceful and calm. Kate liked the way people would stop to admire the great Tower of London. The place made her feel proud to be English.

As the pair walked over the old cobbled streets around the Tower, Leon asked Kate if she would like to stop for a glass of wine in the local pub. Kate agreed and found a seat outside the Tiger whilst Leon was getting the drinks.

It was nice to sit down and admire the pub's surroundings – the pub was a little piece of Tudor England against the modern backdrop.

'Here you are, Kate.'

'Thanks, Leon.'

'Look, Kate, I have something serious to tell you.'

Kate looked puzzled. She wasn't accustomed to such seriousness so early on in a relationship.

'I have to tell you the real reason why I am going to America. I have to go there for an operation on my heart. My left ventricle is blocked and if I don't have it unblocked soon I could die.'

'Oh, I'm sorry to hear that, Leon.'

'No listen, Kate. I have also a good friend coming over there with me, Niva. She is my ex-girlfriend of ten years. We broke up because of her religion and family. But we have remained close friends ever since.

'Oh, I see,' replied Kate, swallowing her hurt.

'But, Kate, there's nothing going on any more. Niva has your number along with my best friend in the States, called James.

15

James and I studied together at UCLA; his father is a doctor, and James will be taking care of me while I'm over there. It will most probably be James that will phone you and let you know how I'm doing. But, hey, listen, Kate, I'm not going until 5 a.m. on Monday so we have the rest of the day and tomorrow to enjoy together.'

'I know, Leon,' said Kate, disappointed. 'But I cannot believe that I could be losing you so soon, just as I am getting to know you.'

'I'll keep you informed, Kate. You have no need to worry. Anyway, fancy another glass of wine?'

'Yes please.'

Kate didn't know what to make of all of this. She began to lose all sense of rationality. Nothing seemed important any more. All of a sudden this man had come into her life, and stolen her heart, only for her to find out that he might not be alive at the end of the week. She felt remorseful and disappointed by this news and she couldn't help but wallow in self-pity.

What Leon had told her over the last few days she didn't know whether to believe or not: the notion that he and his family were not that close, and his ex-wife had forbidden him to have contact with his children by taking them to Scandinavia where she later remarried.

'Cheer up, Kate. Anyone would have thought someone had just died. Here's your glass of wine.'

'Thanks, Leon.'

The once-beautiful day now seemed to have lost all its shine. Things were a little bit awkward between them now.

Kate started to question Leon all about his problems. Leon, not being very co-operative, did all he could to avoid answering her.

Is he telling the truth? thought Kate, or did he say all that because he doesn't want to be with me?

'Did I tell you I can play the guitar?' asked Leon cheerfully after a long period of silence between them.

'Oh, was that your guitar in the corner of the living room?'

'Yes, so when we get back, I'll play you a song if you want. I know Tom will be away all this weekend so we can have a romantic night in.'

16

'That sounds lovely, Leon.'

After a couple of hours in the pub at the Tower of London, Kate and Leon made their way back to Fulham Broadway and to the flat via the District line at Tower Hill tube station.

En route Leon suggested to Kate that they went shopping in the local supermarket to buy the evening meal. Kate had a great taste in wine, and was happy to choose the appropriate bottle that would go with the food.

Back in the flat, Kate helped Leon put the shopping in the cupboards. Leon managed to reach up and uncork a bottle of red wine. He brought it into the living room with the glasses and poured the wine for himself and Kate.

Then Leon went over to the corner of the room to get the guitar, which was in desperate need of tuning. He wasn't sure of the correct pitch and he asked Kate if she wouldn't mind tuning it for him. Then he started playing and singing Irish folk songs.

Kate was impressed. 'You should have been a professional folk singer,' she exclaimed.

'I wanted to at the time,' replied Leon, 'then I met and married Susanna, to my family's disapproval. So having made her pregnant, we left for the States for me to pursue a career in medicine. Can you play the guitar?'

'I'll have a go.'

Kate then took the guitar and started to play around with it. She also showed Leon how to go about tuning it properly. He was amazed at her sheer musicality and the fact that she could just pick up an instrument and play tunes.

'You're a real musician,' he said enviously.

'Well I'm not a liar, Leon,' snapped Kate.

Leon didn't know how to take that statement. He knew he had lied to Kate, but didn't know how to undo it. It was as if he was living out his own fantasies which had no ending.

'Well I'm now going to put the dinner on, Kate.'

'I'll come and give you a hand if you would like.'

'That will be great.'

Kate began chopping up the vegetables whilst Leon cooked the pepper steaks. In the kitchen there seemed to some kind of closeness between the two of them which Kate liked.

Yet deep down Kate knew it was going to be hard with the uncertainty about Leon's health. Hopefully the operation would be a success so that he could live out the rest of his life with very few heart problems or none at all.

It didn't take Kate and Leon very long to prepare dinner.

Over dinner Kate began to reminisce about her childhood and Leon likewise. She loved the way he spoke of his native Ireland. Especially of the countryside, and the bridge over the river Ardee that ran into the hills. Kate sensed a kind of serenity in his voice when he spoke of the past.

He also spoke of his parents, and how hurt and angry he was with his dad. When he was only fifteen years old, his dad left the family home. And it was since then that Leon had begun to despise him, especially since it left his mother in a bad way.

Leon's family were quite well known in Ireland in horse racing circles. His brother David was a jockey and raced in many national competitions. He was proud of his brother, until the day he was caught gambling and fixing race meetings with top American and Japanese business tycoons.

This led to David fleeing Ireland when the officials found out. He set up home in Maryland, America, where he ran a riding school.

Kate helped Leon tidy up after dinner. Leon suggested going out but Kate hoped that they could stay in and be all romantic. Seeing it was their last night together, she reluctantly agreed to go with him to his local on the King's Road.

Kate felt a little uneasy about drinking in this pub. The atmosphere didn't feel very welcoming. She would have much preferred to have had a romantic night in instead. Yet considering that he might die, it may be the last time he drinks in here.

Later that evening Kate and Leon walked back home. Kate wasn't at all feeling very romantic. Neither was Leon.

'Kate, I'm going to have to phone James's dad in the States.'

'That's all right.'

'And I have something to tell you or shall I say ask you after I have spoken to him.'

Kate seemed rather surprised. While on the phone he held Kate close to his chest on the sofa.

During their conversation he had with his friend's dad, Leon was happy. They spoke of many things, and one was his journey to the States. Funny though, there hadn't been a date mentioned, thought Kate as she continued to listen to their conversation.

Soon Leon was off the phone.

'Well, Kate, darling, there are various things I need to tell you and it's about you. You have made an enormous impact on my life. If it wasn't for you I would have taken an overdose and committed suicide. I don't want to go to the States to have this operation alone, and knowing that I may not survive at the end of it is scary. Thank you, Kate, for giving me a reason to live.'

Kate felt touched by all this. She didn't know what to say.

'Also, Kate, I want you to be my wife. Will you marry me?'

'Yes, Leon, I will.'

Then Leon and Kate started to make plans about their wedding. Kate felt happy. Leon was the first man to ever ask her to marry him after only a couple of weeks. Everything seemed to be moving so fast.

'I'll buy you an engagement ring in America,' said Leon. 'What would you like?'

'Diamonds and rubies as the stones and 18 carat gold.' Kate grinned.

'Very well, diamonds and rubies you shall have, my darling.'

For that moment Kate was absorbed with the future, yet deep down she had her doubts. She thought, he may have forgotten he's having an operation or maybe knowing that she was going to be his future wife might give him the will to live.

'Well, I think it's time for bed. Are you tired, Kate?'

'Yes, I am rather,' she replied, and followed Leon into the bedroom.

Chapter Four

Kate could hardly sleep a wink all night. Everything seemed strange and she felt bewildered.

'Leon,' said Kate softly. 'Did I recall rightly that you asked me to marry you last night?'

'Yes,' replied Leon; 'you're not having any doubts, are you?'

'Oh no, Leon. I'm just making sure after a night's sleep that you're still interested in marrying me.'

'Of course, darling. Come here.'

Kate moved closer to Leon, he began to embrace her tightly. In his arms, Kate felt safe and secure. It was a feeling that she did not want to lose.

It took a long while for Kate and Leon to stir from the bedroom. Kate woke up first and ran the bath for her and Leon to share. Then she went into the kitchen and made Leon a cup of tea. As she was doing it, Leon got up to phone James in the States to confirm his arrival the following morning.

Kate felt a bit down. She wished that she could have gone with him to help him through this. But on the other hard she knew that she had to be strong and not let this get in the way of what could effectively be their last day together. For a while anyway!

'Well, darling,' said Leon as he put his arms around Kate, 'what shall we do today?'

'How about going for a picnic?'

'That sounds marvellous, Kate. Let's have a bath, get dressed and go into town to get some food. Then go to Regent's Park to eat it.'

After they had had a bath and got dressed, Leon and Kate then made their way to the shops to pick up some food – a French stick, along with a selection of cheeses, pâté, and a bottle of white wine – before getting the number eleven bus from Fulham Broadway to take them into Oxford Street to get another bus to Regent's Park.

It was a lovely hot day, perfect for a picnic. Kate found a quiet spot by the lake.

'Let's sit here,' she exclaimed.

'All right, this is quite nice.'

Then they began to indulge themselves with the delicious food and take full advantage of the surroundings. The park was quite busy; there were lots of tourists walking around, also taking advantage of the beautiful day and the park. It was hard to believe that whilst sitting in the park, one was actually in London.

'Well, Kate, I think it's time to start heading back.'

'Okay.'

Kate helped Leon to pack away their rubbish before heading towards Regent's Park tube station to get the Bakerloo line to Paddington Station. Then they got the Circle line to Edgware Road before changing for the District line to Fulham Broadway. They arrived back in Fulham in no time.

'Kate.'

'Yes, Leon.'

'I think it would be best if we said our goodbyes.'

'I suppose so. Well, I hope everything goes all right.'

'Kate, don't worry. James has your number and will keep you informed of everything.'

'Yes, well, take care and I'll see you soon.'

'Definitely.'

Then Leon kissed Kate on the lips. They embraced for what seemed quite a while.

'See you, Kate.'

'Bye.'

As Leon walked slowly away from her, Kate stood frozen on the spot at the entrance of the tube station. She suddenly felt totally alone. It seemed ages since she had been alone. It was strange. Kate didn't know how to deal with it.

She soon pulled herself together, and phoned Jane from the station payphone beside the ticket office in the entrance hall.

'Hello, Jane.'

'Hello, Kate. How are you?'

'Oh I'm all right, I suppose. But the reason why I am phoning you is to see if you are free today.'

'Of course, Kate, why don't you come on over?'

'Okay. I'll see you in about half an hour.'

'No problems. I'm at home all alone so I'll see you when you get here.'

Kate then got back on the tube to Liverpool Street and caught a bus to take her to Stoke Newington where Jane lived. Kate couldn't wait to see Jane and tell her all that had been happening between her and Leon.

Then the doubts started to set in. Leon had managed to pull Kate into his own dream world. She had begun to lose all sense of reality. It was like she was playing a part in a film and it would be all over in a second.

But it wasn't, all her emotions had been turned upside down. This she couldn't deal with. Nothing seemed rational any more. Maybe it was, but Kate couldn't connect with what was rational and what was irrational.

Jane had her way of bringing Kate back to reality. Even when they were at college together Jane helped her through the difficult times, especially when she lost her voice and could no longer sing opera. Jane helped her to see reality, and that was what made her a best friend.

Kate soon arrived at Jane's house. Jane was really pleased to see her.

'How are things?'

'Oh, Jane, I don't know where to begin.'

'It's good to see you, Kate. Here, have a glass of wine, and you can tell me all about it.'

'Thank you, Jane. That would be nice.'

Jane handed Kate a glass of red wine. Then Kate began to tell Jane all about Leon, the operation in America and the proposal of marriage. Jane seemed puzzled by it all.

'Kate,' Jane interrupted.

'Yes, Jane.'

'Things seem to be moving at a very fast pace. Are you sure you're really happy, because you don't seem it?'

'Oh, I don't know, Jane. I really don't know what to make of him and all of this. He told me he was married with kids, and about how one of his children was killed in a car crash. Then he told me all about Niva, who he is still close with. He isn't with her now because her father and her religion won't allow it. So you see, I really don't know what to make of it all.'

'Well, Kate, for now just forget about it. You're more than welcome to stay here in the spare room. Darren is away so we could go out, just the two of us, like we used to.'

'All right.'

Kate and Jane then got ready to go out. They made their way to the local pub on the corner of Church Street, just around the corner from Jane's flat. When they arrived it was really busy. As Kate waited for Jane to get the drinks some strange man came over to talk to her. Kate was quite flattered but turned down his advances.

Jane was glad that they had decided to go out as this helped Kate take her mind off Leon.

'Thanks, Jane, for dragging me out.'

'That's all right, Kate. I needed to get out as well and what better way to do it than with my best friend.'

'Well, Jane, it's closing time in a few minutes and I'm feeling tired.'

'Yes, I am rather. Let's go home.'

Kate and Jane then made their way back to the flat.

'So I'll see you in the morning, Jane, and thanks for tonight.'

'No problems. See you in the morning, and don't worry, everything will be fine.'

Chapter Five

Kate woke up still in disbelief. She somehow couldn't face today knowing that Leon would now be in America.

Jane was sympathetic. But right now Kate felt totally alone and empty. It was like she was already mourning him.

'How are you feeling today?' asked Jane chirpily.

'Oh, I'm fine.'

'Really, Kate?'

'No, but I just have to be,' said Kate in a rather aggressive manner. 'Anyway, thank you, Jane, for putting me up. I am going to have to go back home to Orpington for a few days as I have *Sanctus Christe* to finish off.'

'All right, Kate; look, just call me when you hear something.'

'I will.'

Kate then got the bus from Jane's house to London Bridge, where she was to get her train to Orpington. All Kate could do to get her mind off Leon was to throw herself wholeheartedly into her work. She started to miss him, she hoped that he or one of his friends would call her to let her know how he was doing. But no one did.

Three days later the phone rang. It was Leon. Kate jumped out of the bed with joy.

'Hello, Kate. How are you?'

'I am fine.'

'What are you doing?' quizzed Leon.

'Well, I've just got out of bed to answer the phone, Leon, as it is two o'clock in the morning over here. What time is it over in America, and how did your operation go?'

'Well, Kate, I am not in America. I'm back in Chelsea watching a late night film, and I didn't need an operation in the end.'

'You didn't?'

'No, Kate, they just gave me an injection to unblock it and that was that. But the reason why I came straight back is because I am missing you. Kate, can I see you?'

'Of course. I am missing you too.'

'No, Kate, I really need to see you. Can you leave for London straightaway?'

'I wish I could, Leon, darling, but there are no trains running at this time of the night. I will see you tomorrow at 7 a.m.'

'Please, Kate, as I'm so looking forward to seeing you again.'

Then Leon hung up. Kate was puzzled. She couldn't sleep after he had phoned her. She was completely wide awake. As she lay in bed, all sorts of questions were beginning to enter her mind. Did he really go to the US? Did he really have an operation? What if he is lying?

These were all the questions that were plaguing her. Yet in the end she just dismissed them by thinking he probably was telling the truth; after all he was a doctor. Doctors never lie!

Soon morning had arrived. Kate had overslept and did not wake up until ten o'clock. She felt guilty that she had not been to see Leon at the flat before now. Just as she was about to get the train to London, Leon phoned.

'Where are you, Kate?'

'I'm at Orpington Station.'

'Will you meet me in the Sussex Arms in Covent Garden at three o'clock?'

'All right, I'll meet you there at three. See you later.'

'Yes. Bye.'

Kate suddenly felt nauseous. She didn't know what to expect or what kind of state he would be in. Basically she didn't know whether he would be drunk or sober. This was the first time she had felt like this about Leon. Was she now bearing witness to his strange behaviour and realising he was not all that he made out he was?

Soon it was three o'clock. Leon glanced out of the window to see Kate approaching the pub. Then he went to the door to greet her.

'You look wonderful,' he complimented her. 'I missed you so much, Kate. Here, I've bought you some pink carnations.'

'Oh, Leon, they are wonderful. Thank you.'

After Leon had ordered Kate a glass of red wine from the bar, they began to kiss and embrace.

'I'm so glad you're still alive and looking well,' exclaimed Kate.

'Yes, I am. Now I can spend my time with you.'

Leon began to tell Kate all about the supposed trip to the States.

'Well, Kate, let's go back and have something to eat.'

'That would be lovely, as I haven't eaten anything much today.' On the way back to Chelsea, Leon stopped in the local delicatessen to get some food, and a bottle of red wine.

Kate was happy to be back with him, holding his hand and feeling close to him. This she yearned for, and had missed for three days.

'Kate, my sister is over from Ireland for the summer and she is working in London. I've told her all about you and she wants to meet you.'

'That sounds lovely. When did she say she will be free?'

'I told her that we will meet her at South Kensington station at two o'clock tomorrow; she is working in a boutique close by. I can see you two getting on really well.'

'What's she called?' asked Kate.

'Her name is Sinead; she is twenty-four years old and looks very much like me.'

'I see. Well, I'm really looking forward to meeting her.'

Kate and Leon began to reacquaint their bodies. When they got into the flat, Leon took Kate's hand and led her to the bedroom where they got undressed. Leon then began to massage her and caress her into making love. Kate, hungry for him, continued to reciprocate his advances and they were deep in passion all night.

Leon never really got a chance to cook for Kate, as their appetites were certainly consumed with love for one another.

Chapter Six

Morning had soon arrived. The birds were singing away. Then the phone rang. Leon hastily got up to answer it. When he came into the bedroom he didn't look very happy.

'Look, Kate, that was the hospital. I have to go into work; why don't you go and meet my sister?'

'I would like to, but I don't know what she looks like.'

'Well, do what you want,' snapped Leon. 'Here is her number, give her a call. I've got to go.'

Leon then got dressed and started to make his way to work.

'Okay, love, see you later,' shouted Kate.

'Yeah, well, I'll call you.'

Kate suddenly felt dismayed. It was like he had become a different person. One she hadn't noticed before. He was very distant and Kate was quite offended by it.

Was Leon now beginning to show his true colours? She didn't know what to make of it all.

Kate eventually got out of bed, had a bath and then decided to phone Sinead, as well as Jane. Jane was quite curious about Leon and started to have her suspicions about him.

'Look, if you want me to be around when you meet her I will,' said Jane.

'No, Jane, I will have to meet her on my own. It is the only way I will ever find out the truth about him.'

Kate agreed to meet Sinead at South Kensington station. On the phone she gave Kate a clear indication of what she looked like. Kate liked the way she sounded over the phone and wasn't at all nervous about meeting her.

Kate left Leon's place and began to walk towards Fulham Broadway. It was a lot busier than usual at the ticket office. Kate got her ticket and got onto the train to South Kensington.

When she finally got there, she found Sinead waiting for her. Sinead was wearing blue denim jeans, and a blue tunic top. She had short dark hair and carried a black shoulder bag.

'Hello, Kate.'

'Hello, Sinead. I'm so pleased to meet you.'

'Likewise,' replied Sinead.

Sinead then took Kate to a wine bar in South Kensington. It seemed really nice inside. It was very bright and open-plan, and also very expensive.

Sinead ordered a bottle of red wine. She figured Kate would need it after she had told her what her brother was really like.

'Well, Kate, I'm so pleased to meet you, especially on your own. So how do you cope with my brother?'

'With great difficulty at times. He has just come back from the States and it seems like this heart operation has changed him.'

'Oh dear, Kate, is that what he told you?' asked Sinead, rather disappointed. 'I'm afraid to tell you he wasn't in America having an operation on his heart. He doesn't have heart trouble. The trouble he has is that he went on an alcohol binge. He is an alcoholic! What other lies has he told you?'

'Well,' replied Kate rather slowly and gulping down half a glass of wine in order to contain her shock, horror and disbelief. 'He says that he is a doctor working as a locum for London hospitals, and that he had been married to a woman called Susanna who gave birth to his two children, one of whom died in a car crash. Then there is his good friend Niva whose dad is a rich Arab and wouldn't let them get married.'

'Kate,' Sinead paused, 'this makes me so angry. I think you ought to know the truth. He is not a doctor, he is a gym instructor working in Soho at some posh club. And he has never been married nor has he any children. But I'm afraid to tell you all that he says about Niva is true.'

Kate looked upset. Sinead could sense that and poured more wine into her glass. There was then an awkward silence between them. Kate didn't know what to make of it all, or how to handle all of this.

'Kate, if I were you,' said Sinead sympathetically, 'I would get the fuck away from him. He will only drag you down, like he did to his other girlfriend Lisa.'

'What happened to Lisa?' asked Kate.

'About thirteen years ago Leon left Ireland to set up home with her in London. She helped him to get a job and was also providing for them both, while Leon, instead of going to work, was drinking. Lisa began to question him and he started beating her up. Niva was the only one Leon ever really loved, because she has got money to fund his alcoholism. If it wasn't for her he would be living on the fucking streets. This is also one of the reasons why he is still close to her.'

'So do you think they are still having an affair?'

'No, Kate, but he will never stop seeing her. I know how this must all seem to you, Kate. I am only saying this for your own good, because I don't want to see you end up like Lisa. Left for dead and downright broken-hearted.

'Look, now you know the truth only you must decide what you want to do. He is my brother and I love him. But I hate the way he treats people, especially women that are close to him. Well, I must go now, Kate. Think about what I said. You know you can always give me a call. But believe me darling, one of the reasons why I try and avoid seeing him is because he is fucked up. Take care. Bye.'

'Bye, Sinead.'

Kate felt depleted.

Oh dear, thought Kate. What am I going to do except confront him with the truth. The lying bastard. How could he do this to me?

Then just at that point her phone rang. It was Leon. 'Can you meet me at Oxford Street station in one hour?' he asked rather anxiously.

'Yeah. Okay.' Then Kate hung up.

Kate left the wine bar and decided to get the bus there. She stopped off in a wine bar quite close to Oxford Circus, and ordered three glasses of white wine which she drank in quick succession. And then she made her way to the once love of her life, to the complete tosser from hell who would be waiting for her outside the station by Shelley's shoe shop.

Kate felt slightly drunk. She had to be. She felt nothing but anger. Mainly the anger was directed towards herself for allowing herself to be easily fooled by a complete wanker such as Leon

McCarthy.

When she arrived, Leon was waiting for her like prey. He was pleased to see her but sensed that something was wrong with her.

'Hello, Kate, darling.'

'Oh. Hi, Leon,' said Kate rather casually. 'I see that you have now managed to cheer yourself up, you fucking lying bastard.'

Leon felt threatened by Kate's tone. He instantaneously grabbed Kate's neck with his right hand and began to squeeze it.

'If you don't want me to break it, sweetheart, you'd better fucking listen to me. You don't ever shout at me in public again,' said Leon menacingly.

'I'm sorry, Leon. Will you let go of my neck – you are hurting me!'

'Good. Now let's go to the Sussex Arms, and we'll talk over a pint of lager, which you are going to drink with me. Then I shall see you back onto the train to Orpington.'

Kate felt like crying. Leon could see it in her eyes. She knew that if she did cry, this could provoke him even more into hurting her.

Once in the pub, Leon got the drinks whilst Kate found an empty table to sit at. Then Leon began to ask Kate what was said in the meeting she had had with Sinead. When Kate told him, he paused.

'It's all true,' replied Leon slowly. 'The only reason why I stay with you is because of your talent as a musician. I think that is incredible. But to be honest with you I find you a psychotic, mentally disturbed person, and I think you need psychiatric help. I thought we could be really good together, but you had to spoil it. You and my sister. I hope you are happy. Have a good life.'

Leon then drank his pint in one and walked away. Kate was left feeling totally depleted and mortified.

'Oh God help me,' cried Kate inside.

Still hurting from the wrath of Leon, she managed to get the train back to Orpington and out of London. A British Transport policeman who saw the incident between Leon and her outside Oxford Street station began to follow her as she boarded the tube alone to Tottenham Court Road where she picked up the

Northern line to Waterloo, to offer Kate support.

Kate rejected it and carried on home.

Chapter Seven

Now back in Orpington, Kate felt relieved. Deeply heartbroken and distraught, she continued to finish *Sanctus Christe*, and began work on a new composition, *Deum Et*.

Deum Et was a complete contrast to her other works, full of dashing harmonies, twisted textures, and a fiery mood which raged in the middle, before a sense of peace arrived. This could be seen as Kate's second best work.

Physically hurt and heartbroken, Kate's body was like a shell. She was just existing.

Then at twelve o'clock Kate decided to phone Leon. She knew it would be a mistake. But somehow she felt compelled to phone him. At least if she talked with him it might make her feel better.

'Hello, Tom. It's Kate. Is Leon there?'

'Oh, I'm sorry, Kate. He is not. He has gone back to Ireland. His mother has passed away, and he hasn't told me when he will be back.'

'Okay, Tom. Thanks. Bye.'

'Bye, Kate.'

Kate, already exhausted by it all, began to feel sorry for him. She couldn't believe that his mother had suddenly passed away.

He wouldn't lie about that, would he? thought Kate. I will soon find out as I will phone his sister up in the morning.

Kate seemed obsessed by him. It was as if she enjoyed him torturing her. What if this was a ploy to win her back? If it was, it was rather a sick way of doing it. That was of course if he did fake it and lie about the whole thing.

Kate awoke rather restless. She phoned Sinead but there was no answer. She even tried to phone him in Ireland, and there was still no answer.

Then, Kate remembered that he called his brother Phillip up after a rugby match using her mobile. It took Kate ages to look on her itemised phone bill for his mobile number. Eventually she found it.

When she tried phoning him the answer machine was on, so she left a message. But despite that, Kate still kept on trying until she got hold of him. Phillip was surprised to hear from her.

He thought that something serious had happened to Leon, and that was the reason for her phoning him. But then when she told Phillip what had happened, he couldn't believe it. He sounded very distraught. It was like he never knew. Phillip then made some excuse to hang up.

It all started to sound strange. Was he really lying?

Then Sinead phoned Kate up, and asked her what Leon had said. When Kate told her Sinead replied, 'I'm sorry, Kate. Our mother is not dead. She is very much alive. In fact she has only just arrived in London and is staying with me for a while. The reason why she is over here is to get him back home to Ireland, so he can go to a rehab hospital to sort himself out. But I think that is an impossible task. Look, Kate, if he does call you let me know, won't you? It's just that I need to get him to see mum face to face. Will you do that for me?'

'Yes,' answered Kate, 'I will.'

'Kate, I must go. Phone me.'

After the conversation with Sinead, Kate felt numb. 'How could I have allowed myself to fall for such an evil, cruel, nasty man?' she cried. 'What have I done to have deserved this? Was it to make me a better person or was it a way of getting back at me for all the trouble I may have caused in the past?'

Kate decided to pull herself together. She phoned Jane and her agent. Her agent Alan was pleased to hear from her and so was Jane. Yet Jane noticed the difference in Kate's tone over the phone. Jane couldn't help but worry about her friend. She knew that something had happened between Leon and Kate so she invited Kate to stay for a few days.

Kate, agreeing to Jane's invitation, packed her bags and headed back up to London, along with her new musical compositions, *Sanctus Christe* and *Deum Et*.

Kate couldn't wait to see Jane and her agent Alan. She knew Alan would be pleased with her new work, and would also be happy that she had finally finished *Sanctus Christe*. It seemed to have taken her ages to write. The work was written for choir and orchestra, and the London Symphony Orchestra and choir would be performing it at the end of June.

Soon Kate got into London Bridge and Jane was already waiting for her outside W H Smiths.

'Hello, darling,' said Jane, giving Kate a big hug. 'Are you all right?'

'No, Jane, but I am glad that I can stay with you for a few days. I have a meeting with my agent Alan in an hour. I would love you to come with me to the Barbican, otherwise I'm only going to break down.'

'Okay, Kate. Let's go.'

On the way to the Barbican, Kate began to tell Jane everything that had happened so far between Leon and herself. Jane, although surprised, could believe it. Somehow she knew the night that Kate first met Leon that something wasn't right about him. A gut feeling deep down made Jane realise he wasn't to be trusted and that there was something very sinister about him.

'Oh, Kate, I wish I had never had a birthday party in that wine bar.'

'Well, Jane, it cannot be helped.'

Soon Kate and Jane found themselves at the Barbican. Alan's office was only around the corner from the tube station. His office was beside a small law firm. One had to go up a flight of stairs to get to it. Once inside Alan greeted them both and that made Kate better again.

'Well, Kate, I thought I had given up hope on you when you hadn't been in touch. So how are you both?'

'Very well,' replied Jane. Kate didn't answer.

'Alan, I have bought two new works, one of which was never commissioned, but I figured will be an instant hit.'

'Really, Kate, do you have the manuscript, and a working record of it?'

'Yes, Alan, here it is. *Sanctus Christe* and *Deum Et.*'

Alan took the manuscript and the recordings of the works. He put them into the stereo system that was sitting on the shelf and began to play the works. *Sanctus Christe* was played first, then *Deum Et.*

Alan and Jane seemed slightly disturbed by her uncommissioned work *Deum Et*, but they also liked it. The rhythmic patterns were disjointed over the twisted textures. The melodies were very distant and unmelancholic.

'Kate, this work is brilliant. This has to be your best work yet,' exclaimed Alan. 'What have you been up to to have created such a piece of music?'

'Oh, Alan, you don't want to know,' replied Kate, 'Well, anyway, we must be going.'

'I fully understand, Kate. I will call you when the London Symphony Orchestra agrees to rehearse this, but I will see you at the first rehearsal anyway of *Sanctus Christe*. A date yet to be confirmed.'

'Okay, Alan. I will speak to you soon.'

'Goodbye, Kate. Jane.'

'Bye, Alan,' replied Jane.

On the way back to her house, Jane called into the off licence to get a bottle of champagne.

'What's that for, Jane?'

'This is for you, so that it will cheer you up, because that work *Deum Et* is bloody marvellous, and you deserve a lot of good luck at the moment.'

'Thanks, Jane.'

'So put him at the back of your mind. If I hear his name again today I will charge you a pound. We are going to celebrate you tonight.'

'Great,' exclaimed Kate. 'Let's drink.'

Then Kate and Jane headed back to the flat.

Chapter Eight

After a week without Leon, Kate was beginning to feel a lot happier. She hoped he would have phoned her during that time, but no such luck.

Sinead had phoned Kate the day before to see if she had heard from Leon. Yet fortunately for Kate she hadn't, or rather not until now – two o'clock in the morning.

'Hi, Kate. It's Leon.'

'Oh, hi, Leon. Where are you?'

'I'm back in Chelsea.'

'Oh, I see.'

'Look, Kate, I really miss you. Can I see you tomorrow please?'

'What for?'

'Well you do have stuff over here, and I think we need to talk.'

'What time?'

'As soon as you can get over here.'

'All right, Leon, I'll meet you at eight in the morning.'

'Okay, Kate. I'll see you then.'

'Bye.'

'Bye, Kate, till tomorrow.'

Kate began to feel nervous about meeting him. She didn't know what to expect. Would he be drunk? What more lies would he tell?

Yet pondering on all of this wouldn't make things any easier. She still had to face him and that was the hardest part.

Eight o'clock soon arrived. She was feeling rather nauseous. Kate couldn't believe that she was about to meet Leon. Jane would be angry with her if she knew. So she did her best not to let on to her why she had to leave her house early.

As Kate approached Leon's place, she paused on the corner of the street before knocking on the door.

'Hi, Kate. I am so pleased to see you.'

'Hello, Leon. I can't say likewise, but anyway how are you?'

'I am fine, Kate. Look, I have really missed you. Let's give it another go, please.'

Then Leon grabbed Kate's waist, and began to hold her, kiss her neck, and caress her.

Kate, feeling aroused, started to miss the feeling that Leon was so good at giving her. She wished deep down that he had never started this. But he carried on until Kate finally agreed to give him one last chance.

'Okay, Leon. You win, but why, why, why do you torment me so? I cannot believe I'm agreeing to give you one last chance. Jane and everyone will kill me. Look, Leon, you're going to have to phone your sister – she is worried about you.'

'I will, Kate, but not today. Let's go out for the day, and get re-acquainted again.'

'Where?'

'How about Tower Bridge, and take it from there?'

'All right, Leon.'

Leon and Kate then began to make their way to Fulham Broadway tube station. Leon bought two one day travel cards and headed down to the tube platform for the district line to Tower Bridge.

Kate liked Tower Bridge. She felt at ease there, and it gave her inspiration, helping her to reach her innermost thoughts and feelings. Sometimes she would find them disturbing. But it did help her get in tune with her own creativity.

Leon was behaving like the way he did when they first went out, charming, witty and nice. It was this that finally convinced her to take him back. She didn't have the heart to finish with him. Yet little did Kate know, this wasn't going to last. In fact, going back out with Leon was the worst thing she could do.

Arriving at Tower Bridge, Leon took Kate's hand and walked with her to the bridge, where they picked up the path that was alongside the river. It was very busy. Tourists were everywhere. Especially the number of tourists taking pictures. Kate and Leon found it hard not to walk through the group photographs being taken and spoil their shots.

Kate felt relieved that Leon and she were getting on better, laughing and joking like they used too.

'When we get home, Kate, I'm going to cook you one of my specialities just for a gorgeous and talented lady. Then I am going to serenade you.'

'That sounds lovely, Leon.'

'Come on. Let's go, Kate.'

Back on the tube to Fulham, Leon couldn't leave Kate alone. They were kissing and cuddling all the way home. Kate enjoyed this. It was the only thing she had seemed to have missed.

When they arrived back at the flat, Kate started to help Leon prepare the dinner. Leon cooked the chicken whilst Kate prepared the salad and vegetables.

'Do you remember the first meal you ever cooked me, Leon?'

'Yes, I do. I will never forget that night I first met you. I'm sorry about all the things I said to you, really I am.'

'I forgive you, Leon.'

But you really did hurt me too. Knowing that I was losing you as a friend as well as a lover.

'So why did you do it, Leon?'

'I don't know, Kate. It's just that I have been so hurt in the past, that I just keep putting this barrier up, and I'd rather hurt other people than face up to my own problems.'

'So why did you lie about your mother's death?'

'I know, Kate. I'm sorry, but I had to do something in order to get away from it all and hurting you was the last thing I wanted to do.'

'All right, Leon, but you still have a lot of making up to do.'

'Yes, Kate. Come here and give me a kiss.'

'Leon.'

Kate and Leon then embraced. Kate was feeling happier. She didn't want to fall out with Leon. She really did like him.

'Come here. Kate. Let's keep dinner for later, and get an early night. What do you say?'

'Okay, Leon.'

Then Leon took Kate's hand and led her into the bedroom. They both began to strip off seductively. Kate was arousing Leon's emotions as Leon was Kate's. Then in the midst of passion Leon began to fall asleep.

Kate didn't seem to mind too much. She too felt emotionally exhausted by it all and joined him in slumber.

Chapter Nine

When Kate arose from slumber, and saw Leon next to her, she felt content again. Leon was still asleep. Kate was pleased as this gave her a chance to phone up Sinead and set up another meeting, but with Leon and his mum this time.

Sinead sounded pleased to hear from Kate. 'Hello, Kate,' she said joyfully.

'Hi, Sinead. How are you?' replied Kate.

'I am fine. Have you heard from my brother?'

'Yes. I'm with him now. He's in bed asleep.'

'How is he?'

'Oh well, he is very apologetic. Look, how about we meet up?'

'Okay. What about this lunchtime at South Kensington station as usual?'

'Yes that's fine.'

'All right. I'll see you then. Bye, Kate.'

'Bye, Sinead.'

After speaking to Sinead, Kate went into the kitchen to make Leon some breakfast – slices of toast with butter and jam on them and a cup of tea. While Kate was waiting for the kettle to boil, Leon walked into the kitchen and surprised her. He gently put his arms around her waist and started nibbling her ear.

'Hello, Leon, darling.'

'Hello, Kate,' muttered Leon while kissing her neck.

'Why don't you go back to bed? I'll bring the tea and toast through to you in a minute.'

Kate then took the breakfast tray into the bedroom, where Leon was lying waiting for her on the bed.

'Thank you, darling, for this. Why don't you come and lie down next to me?'

'Okay.'

Leon then gentle started to fondle Kate. He started to massage her breasts, arousing her fully until they were making love. Kate

40

loved the way Leon touched her.

Feeling him inside her made her feel really complete. She wished they could keep this going all day. Then Leon climaxed, he carried on until Kate climaxed with him at the same time. This brought a smile to Kate's face.

'Well, I think the breakfast is cold now.'

'Not to worry, Kate. I'm feeling quite hungry now. Thanks for making breakfast anyway.'

'What are your plans for the day?' asked Kate.

'I'm not sure.'

'Well anyway, Leon, I have to go into the city as I have an important meeting at twelve o'clock.'

'Oh, I thought we could have spent it together. Will I see you later?'

'Yes, I'll meet you in the Sussex Arms at about four o'clock. All right?'

Kate then got dressed, and left Leon in bed.

There was no way she could tell Leon the truth about meeting Sinead and his mother. She wanted to but she didn't know how he would react to it. It could have provoked him into attacking her if she did tell him, or into another row.

'Well, Leon, I must go now, see you at four in the Sussex.'

'Yes. See you later.'

Then Kate gave Leon a quick kiss and left him to it.

On the way to South Kensington station Kate started to feel uneasy. She couldn't believe that she had allowed herself to be manipulated by Leon and his family, conspiring to help him sort out his life of lies and alcohol. 'Why am I doing this?' she whispered.

South Kensington station was the next stop. Kate quickly pulled herself together, and she ran up the steps to the entrance hall where Sinead and her mum were waiting.

'Hello, Sinead, Mrs McCarthy.'

'Hello, Kate,' replied Sinead and Mrs McCarthy simultaneously.

Leon's mother was nothing like Kate had expected. In fact she didn't know what to expect. She was quite small with dark mousy coloured hair and blue eyes. She was rather fashionably dressed for a woman in her sixties.

'It's good to meet you at last,' exclaimed Mrs McCarthy. 'I want you to call me Ruth.'

'Likewise, Ruth.'

'Well, how is Leon?' asked Sinead.

'He seemed fine when I left him, but he does not know I'm meeting you here.'

'Good,' said Ruth. 'How about we all go to that cafe across the road.'

'A jolly good idea,' answered Kate.

Whilst in the cafe, Ruth ordered a pot of tea for three, and asked Kate all about herself. When Kate told her all about the fact that she was a composer and an up-and-coming one at that, Ruth was shocked. She couldn't believe that an intelligent woman such as Kate could fall for such an arsehole as her son. An alcoholic liar, a violent and physically wretched man.

As well as telling Kate all about Leon's problems, she also divulged all about Leon's childhood, and began to blame all the problems he had on the break up of her marriage to Leon's father Bert.

Bert also was an alcoholic womaniser and loved to gamble. It seemed Leon was a chip off the old block, so to speak.

Kate seemed surprised to hear what Ruth had to put up with. It appeared Leon was going the same way as his father, acting and treating women like shit, just like he saw his father do to Ruth.

Ruth knew this, and that was the reason why she needed to get him sorted out – to get him into a rehab hospital and give him the opportunity to get psychiatric help, if that was possible! But deep down Kate could see in Ruth's eyes as she spoke, that would never happen.

'Look, Kate, Sinead and I have to go. I would dearly love to meet you again. Meet me outside Fulham station at twelve o'clock tomorrow, will you please; but don't tell Leon. I want to surprise him; will you promise me that?'

'Yes, Ruth. I will see you tomorrow, and see you soon Sinead.'

'Bye,' said Ruth and Sinead simultaneously.

'Bye,' replied Kate.

After they had left, Kate just sat there staring out of the

window, in total disbelief. It was as if she was starring in a movie that at present had no ending. Her heart began to tell her to give him up. But in the back of her mind she knew that this wasn't going to work out. She consciously believed that she was in love with him, and that she was helping him by doing all of this.

Kate soon pulled herself together. She paid the bill and got the Piccadilly line to Piccadilly Circus.

It was now three thirty. She wasn't due to meet Leon until four o'clock, so she decided to take a slow walk to the Sussex Arms in Covent Garden. When she arrived, Leon was already there standing at the bar, drinking a pint of lager.

'Hello, darling. What would you like to drink?'

'Um, just a half of lager, please, Leon.'

Leon then ordered Kate a drink, as she went to find a seat by the window. The pub was quite crowded. Kate had difficulty in finding a seat at first; as she went to sit down Leon came over to join her.

'How long have you been waiting?' asked Kate.

'About two hours; anyway why do you want to know?' replied Leon abruptly.

'No reason, I thought you might have arrived at the same time as me!'

'Oh, did you get everything done that you wanted to?'

'Yes, just about.'

'Look, Kate, I can't let you stay with me tonight, you better go to Jane's house or home.'

'Why, Leon?' quizzed Kate.

'Because I said. Anyway Niva has invited me around to her place tonight for dinner with her and her brother Ahmed.'

'Oh, I see.'

'No you don't see, Kate. I'll call you when I next want to see you.'

'Right, well I'll go now then, as I have a new composition to write.'

'Yes, well, see you.'

'Yes, Leon. See you around.'

Kate felt angry. She quickly drank her drink and stormed out of the pub. She hurriedly made her way to Leicester Square tube station for the Northern line to Waterloo. Kate was devastated, almost in tears.

'Why have I allowed myself to be treated like this, God, why?' cried Kate as she stood waiting for the train at Waterloo.

Once on the train, Kate felt safe again, relieved to be as far away from him as possible. It now began to seem like a game of chess. Kate as the pawn and Leon as the knight. The knight that never leaves his victim until he or she is bled dry.

Was this what Leon was doing to Kate? Or was he the devil's servant out to get her for being good and kind? Who knows, maybe Leon got his kicks out of treating women like shit.

But for Kate, all she could do was to go home back to Orpington, and to try and break herself away from the magnetic tie that seemed to draw her towards Leon. Otherwise she would never be free, and he would always have the upper hand over her, dragging her down until she was in a bottomless pit, where he could kick her even further until she became like the title of her first work, *Te Deum*.

Chapter Ten

Kate woke up feeling subdued. She really didn't want to be involved with Leon any more, except she had promised Ruth that she would see her at twelve o'clock in Fulham and take her to where Leon was staying.

When she arrived, Ruth was already there waiting for her.

'Hello, Ruth.'

'Hello, Kate. Do you know if Leon is still at home?'

'No I don't, but he is probably in bed asleep, as he was intent on getting completely wasted when I left him to go back to Orpington in Kent yesterday evening. I haven't even phoned to see if he is in.

'Okay, Kate, this is what we are going to do. You phone him. If he doesn't answer we will leave it an hour and go for a walk. Then we will try again. If he still doesn't answer, then we will go round to where he is staying. I want you to wait outside for me whilst I talk with him alone. All right.'

'Yes, Ruth.'

Kate then went over to the payphone by the ticket office on the station concourse. There was no answer.

'Don't worry, we will try again in an hour,' said Ruth calmly. 'Let's go for a walk to Tom's flat.'

On the way Kate told Ruth all about what had happened yesterday between herself and Leon. Ruth wasn't at all surprised that he was blowing cold. He needed his alcohol fix. Niva didn't want to see him. He made up that excuse to be drunk and lie to women.

Ruth could see how hurt Kate was. Kate spoke of the plans they had made, and how they were to spend the rest of their lives together. Again Ruth didn't seem surprised, as she had heard it all before with Lisa.

If he was telling the truth about meeting Niva, it would only be talking in her Mercedes, that's where she gave him money to bail him out from further debt.

Leon hadn't been to work for three weeks. Was he still employed? Ruth began to wonder.

'Listen, Kate, it's now one o'clock. Are we near to Tom's flat?'

'Yes, almost. Do you want me to phone him again?'

'No. I'd much prefer to surprise him, if you know what I mean!'

'Okay. Well it's just around this corner, number 24a. I will wait here for you!'

'All right, Kate. I'll meet you here as soon as I have spoken with him.'

'Good luck, Ruth.'

Ruth then walked up the street to number 24a. At first Leon didn't open the door. It wasn't until he heard Ruth calling him that he decided to answer it.

Kate, waiting around the corner for Ruth, started to feel apprehensive. What if he follows Ruth, leading him to me here? thought Kate. I can't believe I am doing this, I've got to be mad.

It seemed like it had taken for ever for Ruth to come out of the flat. Kate soon felt at ease again when she and Ruth were on their own.

'Let's go to a coffee shop and grab a cup of tea,' said Ruth.

'That sounds lovely,' replied Kate. 'There is a lovely cafe close to the tube station.'

'Great. Let's go.'

On the way to the cafe, Ruth told Kate what had happened between them. Ruth had also told Leon how Kate had helped to get her to the flat to see him.

'All Leon did was cry. He seemed to show such remorse.'

'Do you think you could get him to a rehab hospital in Ireland?' asked Kate.

'I don't know, but he does admit that he has a problem.'

Just then Kate's mobile phone rang. It was Leon.

'Thank you for showing my mum where I live,' said Leon sincerely. 'I would really like to see you today, Kate, please, as I am sorry.'

'Oh, all right, Leon. As soon as I have taken your mum back to South Kensington, I'll call around to see you.'

'Okay, Kate. See you soon. I am not feeling very well so I'll be at home all day.'

'See you soon.'

'Bye, Kate.'

'So how was he on the phone?' asked Ruth worriedly.

'Well, he seemed to show remorse like you said. But I still don't know, I'm feeling rather disconcerted by it all.'

'I understand, Kate. Listen, how about we go for coffee another time, as I must leave you to it.'

'All right.'

Kate helped to show Ruth the train she needed to get back to South Kensington. She knew Sinead would be waiting for her.

'Give my regards to Sinead, won't you?'

'I will, Kate. I hope to see you again soon.'

'I do as well, Ruth. Bye for now.'

'Bye, Kate.'

Kate never knew that that would be the last time she would see Ruth.

Now left on her own walking to the flat, Kate felt nervous. What am I going to expect this time?' thought Kate. Is he going to be hot or is he going to be cold? Kate was dreading seeing him. But deep down she had to see him so that between them they could sort this mess out.

When she arrived at Tom's flat, Leon looked awful. He was pale and looking very ill. Kate seemed quite concerned.

'Hello, Kate.'

'Hello, Leon.'

'I am so glad to see you. I am so sorry for the way I treated you yesterday.'

'Well, Leon, have you eaten?'

'No, Kate. I can't stop feeling sick. I'd prefer it if we could stay in. Tom's gone away again for the weekend.'

'All right, Leon, I will stay another night.'

'Thanks, Kate. You are the only thing that keeps me going. I am so pleased that you brought my mum here to see me today, and because of it I cannot wait until we are married.'

'That's okay, Leon, but for now I think we ought to wait a while before we rush into marriage.'

'Yes, I agree.'

'Look, I'm going back to bed as I'm feeling ill. Just make yourself at home, Kate, darling, and I'll see you later.'

'See you later, Leon.'

Kate felt relieved. She was glad of the space, as she didn't know when Leon would change again. She classed him as Dr Jekyll and Mr Hyde. Mr Hyde was certainly a side of Leon's character that she did not want to meet again in a hurry.

Chapter Eleven

Kate had been with Leon for a couple of days now. With no Tom around, Leon seemed fine. He had spent the night drinking a can of Stella Artois until two in the morning, and again stayed in bed until 5 p.m. the following day. But Kate felt quite content with it all.

Had Mr Hyde finally left Leon's character or was there something awaiting around the corner to spark off the destructive disorder in his personality? thought Kate, whilst making herself a cup of tea. Little did Kate know that this something was about to happen when Tom arrived back later.

Kate, sitting on the sofa watching TV, was relieved that there had been no arguments between them up to now. Maybe that was because she kept her distance and said very little to him when he was drinking himself into a stupor.

'Come on, Kate, let's go for a walk, I'm fed up with staying in.'

'Okay, Leon. I'll just get my coat.'

As they left the flat, the pair began to walk down the King's Road. Kate liked walking down the King's Road. It reminded her of being back at college, the place where Kate and her friends used to hang out, surfing the shops for cheap designer clothes for the college parties that used to happen every other weekend after the concerts they had performed in. They were the good old times, thought Kate.

Kate was glad that Leon didn't suggest going into a pub every time they walked past one. Leon reminisced to Kate about the time he spent with Niva, and how they used to hang out all the time around here. He also gloated about the posh restaurants Niva used to take him to.

Kate felt slightly jealous. Every time Niva's name was mentioned, she found it hard not to show it. She had to bite her tongue and listen with very little response. Otherwise it could provoke Mr Hyde in returning and spoil the day for her.

'Look, Kate, I'm feeling hungry. Let's stop off at Ed's diner for something to eat. It's only across the road. What do you say?'

'Yes, great,' replied Kate, rather wearily.

Ed's diner was well known on the King's Road for its ability to cook fantastic American food, as well as the incredibly large portions that they served. It even had an atmosphere that felt American.

Leon ordered two hamburgers, chips and lemonades. Kate was very hungry and luckily the food didn't take long to be prepared and served up.

'This is delicious,' exclaimed Kate.

'Just what the doctor ordered, eh!' grinned Leon.

'Yes,' muttered Kate.

After they had finished the meal, Leon wanted to stop off at the pub down the road from the diner for a drink. Kate reluctantly agreed and followed him into it. She knew that once Leon was inside, that would be it. They would be in there until closing time, and Leon always insisted on Kate drinking with him.

Kate, by now feeling drunk, suggested to Leon that they went back to the flat to watch a movie that was being shown on Sky that she hadn't seen. Leon agreed. But on the way back to the flat, he had to stop off at the off licence to get eight cans of his favourite lager, Stella Artois.

Kate was pleased that he wanted to go back an hour before closing time to watch this movie with her. She had hoped that he would give up drinking alcohol for the rest of the night, but for Leon that was an impossible task.

When they arrived home, Tom was sitting in the living room waiting for Leon to show. He was pleased to see Kate. Tom really liked her. He couldn't help but wonder what a nice person like her was doing with a good-for-nothing person like Leon.

'Hi, Tom. How are you?' asked Kate.

'I'm fine, thank you, Kate. I heard your new work *Sanctus Christe* the other day being rehearsed while I was visiting some associates at the Barbican. It sounds really good.'

'Thank you, Tom.'

Leon was in the kitchen putting all his cans of lager in the fridge. Tom was pleased to speak with Kate alone without Leon.

But he had things to discuss with Leon and that was going to have to be in private.

Tom had nothing but trouble with Leon's late rent and telephone bill payments. He had had enough. Kate could sense there was an uneasy atmosphere between them as soon as Leon entered the living room.

'Leon, do you think I can have a word with you outside?' asked Tom.

'Yeah, no problem, mate,' replied Leon.

'Sorry, Kate, we shall not be long,' exclaimed Tom.

Once they were outside Kate started to feel nervous. Although slightly drunk she felt strong enough to cope with what was going to happen if the result of their conversation together was bad. 'Will this bring back, Mr Hyde?' she whispered, while watching the movie on Sky, *The Piano*.

They had been outside for half an hour. When they arrived Kate could sense that they had been having quite a heated discussion. And it was this that made Kate feel uneasy.

'I'm going to leave you two to it. I'll see you tomorrow, Kate,' said Tom.

'Goodnight,' replied Kate.

As soon as Tom left the room, Leon went to the kitchen to get three cans of lager. Then he came back in, turned the television off and played his favourite CD – Robbie Williams's *Angel*.

'Is everything all right, Leon. What happened between you and Tom?'

'What happened?' replied Leon aggressively. 'He has asked me to leave because of you. You fucking bitch. You think you can just waltz into my life and stay in this flat with me.'

Kate was stunned by this remark. She didn't know what to say. All she could do was keep quiet and listen.

'Because of you, he has asked me to leave. I told you what he was like. Did you believe me, did you? No you fucking didn't, you psychotic little whore!'

'Don't blame me for this,' shouted Kate. 'I'm not the problem, you are. Just look at you, you're nothing but a hopeless lowlife bastard, who doesn't know what a good thing is if it came and bit you on the arse.'

Leon grew really angry. He was shocked that Kate could say such home truths. He didn't know how to handle it, except through aggression and violence.

'Shut up, you fucking bitch, just shut up. You think you are so perfect, but you're nothing but a mentally deranged whore.'

'No, I won't. I want you to listen to me. It's about time I gave back to you the psycho crap you have been feeding me,' replied Kate calmly.

'I said shut up, don't you understand fucking English, you bitch?'

Then Leon started to get violent. He hit her across the face with such force that Kate hit her head on the wall. Then he grabbed Kate's throat as she let out a scream. He proceeded to drag her to the bedroom, not letting go of her throat.

'I will let go of your pretty neck when you learn to shut the fuck up,' said Leon menacingly.

'No, I won't. I don't care any more what you do to me. You're nothing but a vile evil little man who only gets off on hurting women.'

Leon grew really angry. He then started to squeeze her neck and throat until Kate passed out on the bed. She had never felt pain like it and in order for him to stop and not to kill her she had to pass out.

As soon as Kate had passed out, Leon let go of the hold he had on her neck and throat, and went into the living room to drink all the cans of Stella Artois he had bought from the off licence earlier.

Kate now didn't care what he was doing. All she wanted to do was get as far away from him as possible. But for now she lay still on the bed, praying for the morning to come quickly.

Chapter Twelve

Morning couldn't come soon enough for Kate. All she could think about was how to escape from Leon. Getting out of bed was a nightmare – she felt dizzy, her neck and throat were painfully sore. And when she went to the bathroom, she noticed a black eye, and a bruised forehead.

This made her feel very sick. She slowly managed to get dressed away from the bedroom where Leon was lying fast asleep in his drunken state. She walked out of the flat without making her excuses to Tom as to why she was leaving in a hurry.

Once outside Kate felt relieved. She had never been so scared in all her life. She couldn't walk properly and didn't feel like talking to anybody except Sinead. Kate then phoned her. She was her only hope.

Jane wouldn't be as sympathetic, thought Kate. She'll probably shout at me because I went back with him.

Sinead was pleased to hear from Kate. Kate slowly told Sinead what happened to her last night. Attempting to control the flood of tears over the phone, Sinead tried to console her. Not sounding too surprised by Leon's actions, Sinead managed to get Kate to meet her at Fulham station in about half an hour.

'Listen, Kate, I don't want you to go to the police about this, not yet anyway, or go anywhere near the flat. Not until you have seen me, all right?'

'Yes, okay, Sinead, I'll wait for you in the cafe next to Fulham Broadway tube station.'

'Right. I'll meet you there in half an hour, I promise you.'

'See you then, Sinead.'

Taking Sinead's advice, Kate ordered herself a large pot of tea. She didn't feel much like drinking it as she was feeling really dizzy and sick. The thought of swallowing anything made her feel sick.

Sinead was soon in Fulham. She found Kate waiting for her in the cafe with her head down, and looking really awful. That's when the reality of her brother Leon really begin to hit her. She couldn't believe her brother was responsible for how Kate looked, inflicting pain on another human being. Sinead felt like disowning her brother.

He had gone too far this time. After seeing Kate like this, Sinead felt deep down that there was no hope for her brother to get better. And this made her feel very sad.

'Come on, Kate, what really happened?' said Sinead softly.

'Oh, Sinead,' cried Kate. 'I don't know where to begin.'

'How about I get another pot of tea first, then you can tell me, all right?'

'Okay, Sinead.'

Sinead went over to the counter and ordered a pot of tea for two. When she came back, Kate began to tell her everything that happened the previous night. Sinead listened intently.

'Look, Kate, this is what we are going to do. I'll phone him now and get him to meet me at Fulham station. Then I'll meet you back here. Okay?'

'Fine, Sinead.'

'Good. See you later.'

'Yeah. Bye.'

Kate, left on her own again, began to feel numb. She had no thoughts, and felt no emotion. It was as if she was an empty shell. The feelings she once had for Leon no longer existed.

She had to now think of her future and safety. Leon had borrowed two hundred pounds from her. She had also left some of her belongings around where he lived. At the moment she was very nervous about seeing him again. She just wanted to run away and forget all about the whole blasted thing.

Yet in order for Kate to get her stuff and money back, she had to be nice and polite around him. Even if it meant staying at his flat for one more night and then taking some of her belongings back to Kent when she left the next day. Then that was what had to be done.

Over an hour had passed. There was no sign of Sinead. Kate felt relieved that she didn't have to face Leon yet. She managed to drink some of the tea but was still feeling sick.

Then, just as Kate was thinking about ordering another pot of tea, Sinead turned up with Leon. When Leon saw Kate, he realised what he had done. Leon began to feel ashamed, he never knew he was capable of harming anyone as badly as that.

'So, Leon, what have you got to say for yourself?' said Sinead.

'Nothing,' answered Leon. 'Except Kate fell on the way home down the steps to the flat. She banged her head and eye. That is why she has a bruise on her head and a black eye. She was drunk.'

'So you didn't grab her throat at all.'

'No, I didn't. I don't know what she has been telling you, sis, but it's all lies. You must believe me. We are family.'

'Yes, whatever. I think you had ought to talk and sort this mess out. So I am going to stay here and make sure that you both do, amicably.'

Kate couldn't believe what she was hearing. He was even lying to his sister about it all. How could he? she thought, without bursting into tears. Surely she is not going to believe him?

But knowing all about Leon's past lies, Sinead didn't believe a word of it. She could see that he was lying by the way he said it and by his facial expressions.

'I am sorry, Kate, for hurting you. I would like you to stay one more night. Just as friends.'

'Okay, Leon, I'll stay tonight. But I will leave tomorrow and take some of my stuff with me.'

'Thanks, Kate. I need you even more now as a friend.'

Sinead felt relieved that Kate and Leon had sorted things out. She liked Kate a lot. She hated the way Leon was hurting her, so staying as friends was the best option for them both.

'Well, folks, I must be going,' said Sinead.

'Thanks for being here, Sinead,' replied Kate.

'That's okay. I'll see you soon.'

'Yes. Bye,' said Leon and Kate simultaneously.

'I don't feel very well, Leon. I would prefer it if we went back to Tom's flat.'

'No problem, Kate. I am now going to look after you, so don't worry. I am sorry about last night, Kate – I don't know what came over me. I'm really glad that we can be friends. When we get in I'm going to not drink a drop of alcohol tonight and cook you a really superb meal.'

'Thanks, Leon.'
Leon paid the bill before leaving to go back to the flat.

Chapter Thirteen

Kate woke up, not believing that she had decided to stay at Leon's place after he did that to her the previous night and worse that she might even be willing to stay with him as a friend. If she didn't agree to this, Kate knew that deep down she wouldn't be given her money back or given access to claim her belongings that she had left there.

'Well, Leon, I've got as many as my belongings as I can carry. You couldn't lend me thirty pounds so I can get a taxi and a train back to Orpington?'

'Fine, Kate, here you go. I'll call you.'

'Yes, well, I shall try and arrange with you when it will be possible to collect the rest of my things.'

'All right, I'll speak to you soon.'

'Yes, maybe. Well, bye.'

Kate, still suffering from the wrath of Leon, managed to call Jane at Fulham Broadway station to see if she was available to meet her at London Bridge station in an hour.

Jane was pleased to hear from Kate. But deep down she felt that something awful had happened to her by Kate's tone of voice. Despite this Jane was happy to see her friend.

'All right, Kate. I'll meet you in our usual spot at London Bridge station in an hour as suggested.'

'Thanks. Jane. See you then.'

Kate was relieved that she had finally broke free from Leon. She was hurt by it all. If she wanted to live the rest of her life naturally she had to get as far away from him as she possibly could. Even though the hurt was both physical and emotional, Kate knew it was for the best.

As Kate approached W H Smiths at London Bridge station, Jane was already standing there waiting for her. Kate was looking forward to meeting Jane. She couldn't wait to tell her about her future plans, and that Leon would now not be a feature of any of them.

London Bridge was busy as usual – full of commuters either going to work or finishing work. When Jane saw Kate, she couldn't believe it was her at first, she looked really awful – very pale, like snow. Jane knew instantly that Leon had done this to her. All Jane wanted to do now was to help Kate get over him.

'Hello, Kate,' said Jane, giving Kate a big hug.

'Hello, Jane.'

'Come on, let's get you back to my place. I know Leon has done this to you, and I am going to make sure that you never see him again.

'Thanks, Jane, for being a true friend,' replied Kate.

Kate began to feel a lot happier knowing Jane was there supporting her and helping her get over this. It was not going to be easy, not for now anyway.

Jane took Kate back to her place in Stoke Newington. She knew that physically it would only take a few days to get better, but emotionally it could take months.

'Jane, I have something to tell you.'

'What's that?'

'Thanks for being here for me.'

'That's all right.'

Jane then gave Kate a long hug. Kate began to cry.

'The only reason I went back to him was because I thought he loved me and I loved him. Yet deep down I know it was all a farce. I should have left him when I knew he was lying. I don't know why I didn't. Except I lent him two hundred pounds as well as leaving some of my belongings there. I don't know how I could have been so stupid.'

'Kate, I'm glad that you are all right. I am never going to let him hurt you again.

'I know, Jane, but I still need to get the rest of my belongings back and some of the money as well.'

'I realise that, Kate. What we are going to do is wait until he is out of the flat, and then collect them. I am sure Tom won't mind waiting for you to call around and collect them. And I will even come with you.'

'Thanks, Jane.'

Kate stayed with Jane for a few days. Leon tried to phone. Jane realised he would do that and prevented Kate from answering it. She spoke to him instead.

If I let Kate speak to him while she is in this state she will never get over him, thought Jane, I will only let Kate speak to him when she is feeling much stronger and has got over the physical effects of the relationship with Leon. Then I will allow her to speak with Leon and collect the rest of her things. He has already manipulated Kate once, I will be dammed if I am going to let him do it again.

A week had now passed. Kate soon started to look like her old self again – bright, bubbly and cheerful.

'I can't just sit and mope about. I have to finish this whole sorry saga once and for all,' stated Kate.

Jane was pleased.

'I'm going to phone Leon and try to organise with him when it would be convenient to collect the rest of my things.'

'I understand, Kate, but I'm glad you're looking much better. I have been so worried. To help you get through the final stage of the ties with Leon, I will be here offering support.'

'Thanks, Jane, I know I can count on your support.'

Kate then rang Leon. This was one call she wished that she didn't have to make. Leon was pleased to hear from her. He wished he could have spoken with her sooner.

The two of them spoke at length, and Leon eventually agreed on a date and time when Kate could collect the rest of her stuff. The only unfortunate thing was the money. Leon just didn't have the two hundred pounds but was willing to give her back a quarter of that.

Kate was disappointed. She wanted to clear this matter up once and for all. But she realised that she was not going to do this over the phone, yet on the other hand she could not bear to face him. The idea of meeting him again repelled her.

'Look, Kate, I'll be out, but Tom will be in for you to collect your stuff. I'll leave fifty pounds in the bag for you.'

'Okay, Leon. How about I collect the rest of my things later on today, and I hope that we can meet up as friends again one day.'

'I do as well, Kate. See you around.'

'Bye, Leon.'

Kate asked Jane for her help in collecting her things. Jane agreed profusely.

When they had arrived at Tom's flat, Kate was glad to see Tom answering the door and not Leon. Kate had always liked Tom.

Tom was sorry to hear that Leon and Kate had split up. She had also told Tom the real reasons for it. He couldn't believe Leon was like that.

Then the door began to creak. Tom looked away. Kate suddenly realised that Leon was in, and could hear every word that she had said to Tom. Kate then quickly said farewell, picked up the bags and left with Jane, who helped her on to the train back to Orpington.

'Thanks, Jane, for all your help.'

'No problems, just get yourself better, so we can go out again.'

'I will, Jane. Bye.'

'Bye, Kate.'

Jane was glad that this whole sorry episode with Leon was finally over.

Now Kate can get on with the rest of her life, thought Jane, while waving to Kate on the train at London Bridge.

Kate was relieved to be back on the train. It now seemed that the whole sorry affair was now finally over. Despite losing a hundred and fifty pounds, it was worth it.

'No more, I will not let myself be treated like that again,' muttered Kate, reading her book.

But was that chapter closed with Leon? As far as Kate was concerned, yes. Leon had different ideas. He wasn't ready to give up on Kate that easily. He was angry with her because she told Tom what he did to her, and all Leon wanted now was revenge.

The type of revenge that didn't involve killing her, but psychologically making her life hell.

Chapter Fourteen

Kate was now beginning to feel a lot happier. She was glad that Leon hadn't been in contact and had left her alone. Deep down she missed him. She still had feelings for him, but she never wanted to see him again.

Her agent Alan had been in touch to tell her the dates of the rehearsal of her works *Sanctus Christe* and *Deum Et*.

'The first rehearsal is tomorrow, Kate. You will be there? It starts at nine o'clock. So don't be late,' stated Alan.

'Yes, of course, Alan. I'll see you tomorrow,' replied Kate.

'Bye, Kate, until tomorrow.'

'Bye, Alan.'

Then later that evening at 2 a.m. while Kate was asleep, the phone rang. It was Leon.

Oh dear, thought Kate. What does he want now?

'Hello, Leon,' answered Kate.

'Hello, Kate,' replied Leon menacingly. 'I thought I'd give you a little wake-up call, you stupid fucking bitch. I know you told Tom. How could you be so mentally insane? You stupid fucking bitch!'

Kate didn't say a word. She kept the phone away from her ear before hanging up on him.

Leon didn't stop. He just kept on trying to phone her. It took him three attempts to try and say the same thing. Leon was obviously not getting the message that Kate did not want to know, so she just took the phone off the hook and made the most of her night's sleep.

Kate woke up feeling really tired. It was her big day today. The first and only rehearsal of her new works before the concert later on tonight.

Kate didn't feel very much like attending the rehearsal. All the hatred and anger that she thought she had got over just started again. She despised Leon for spoiling her big day. She knew that if she didn't turn up then it would have meant Leon had won, and she was not going to let that happen.

Kate quickly got dressed and headed towards London Bridge and the Barbican concert hall to meet her agent Alan and the London Symphony Orchestra.

'Hi, Alan,' said Kate hurriedly. 'I hope I'm not late!'

'No, Kate, but how are you?' asked Alan.

'I'm all right; a bit nervous I suppose, but I am excited at the same time.'

'Well, this performance is being broadcast live on Radio 3 tonight, and also EMI have been in touch with me in order to make a CD of *Sanctus Christe* and *Deum Et*. It will be recorded during the rehearsal.'

'Great, well, let's get on with it,' smiled Kate.

For the first time in ages, Kate began to feel positive again. The business with Leon had really taken its toll on her. As soon as Alan mentioned the recording, the misery surrounding the phone call she had had with Leon last night had been replaced with excitement and anticipation. This was her big chance and she wasn't going to let an arsehole like that ruin it for her.

The rehearsal and the recording session went really well. Kate, now feeling content and confident, couldn't wait for the evening concert. She was really excited about it.

Then with two hours to go before the concert Kate's mobile phone rang. It was Leon.

'Oh shit!' exclaimed Kate.

'Are you all right, Kate?' Alan quizzed.

'No,' snapped Kate. 'I am just getting over a boyfriend from hell who obviously is intent on ruining my debut. I'll be fine when he stops phoning me and insulting me.'

'Have you been to the police, Kate?'

'No, I don't think it's worth it.'

'Well I do; if he still persistently phones you, I think you should go to the police.'

'Thanks, Alan. I'll be fine, besides I've got my mother to book me a holiday to Europe for ten days on a coach, which evidently leaves in two days. Hopefully by the time I get back he will have got the message.'

'Well, Kate, let's go over to the King's Head pub and grab a bite to eat before the concert.'

'Great.'

Kate liked going to the King's Head pub, which was just around the corner from the Barbican. It felt like her second home. It reminded her of the good times she had when she was a student at the Guildhall School of Music and Drama.

Kate always liked to reminisce about the time when she turned eighteen and had to take part in a second study concert, playing the piano. Kate's good friends who were brass players decided to take Kate to the King's Head pub to celebrate her birthday.

Kate and her friends played this drinking game, knowing that she soon had to play Shostakovitch and Corelli piano pieces. There was no way she could play them drunk. But that was what she did. She turned up on the platform completely pissed on snakebite and black. She later felt really embarrassed. Seven years on she could now laugh about it.

At the end of her performance Kate's friends turned around and said, 'You made Corelli sound like Shostakovitch and Shostakovitch sound like Schoenberg.'

Luckily Kate's piano teacher soon forgot about it, although Kate was never asked to play the piano in the second study concert ever again.

Time was now approaching for the concert. Alan was asked to do a pre-concert talk along with Kate. Kate was feeling incredibly nervous. Alan reassured her enough to give her the confidence to talk about the work.

Jane turned up to hear her best friend's compositions. She was pleased with Kate's achievements, and was glad she was beginning to get on with her life without Leon around.

However, Leon had not finished with Kate. He heard her work on Radio 3, and tried to phone her. Luckily for Kate, she kept her mobile phone switched off.

'What do you think, Jane?' asked Kate.

'It's superb. The audience loved it.'

'Well, Jane, I'm off on holiday to Europe in a couple of days; I'll promise to send you a postcard.'

'You'd better; do you want to come for a drink?'

'No, I am feeling tired. I am going to get the train back to Orpington. I will call you as soon as I get back from Europe.'

'Have fun.'

'Bye, Jane.'

'Bye, Kate.'

'Well, Alan, I will call you when I get back.'

'You'd better, see you soon.'

'Bye, Alan.'

Kate then left the Barbican and made her way towards London Bridge for the train to Orpington. Kate, exhausted and depleted, was relieved that her work had had its premiere in London. What with the world as her oyster, all she had to do was not allow herself to be put down by Leon any more.

Yet despite all of this little did Kate know that Leon was still trying to phone her. She knew deep down that he would be listening to the radio broadcast of her new works. She just didn't want to speak with him, even though she couldn't stop thinking about him.

Kate was really looking forward to her holiday. Her mother booked it so that she could forget all about Leon and allow herself to come back bright and breezy, ready to fight anything, including her critics. And it was this holiday that was going to do it for her.

Chapter Fifteen

Kate, now back in Orpington following her trip around Europe, felt a hundred times better. She had a lot to think about whilst she was away. In the end she had decided to move away from London and make a fresh start in the north.

Kate saw a job advertised in Scotland as a composer in residence based at Edinburgh University in an English newspaper in Salzburg, Austria. Kate then phoned up her agent to sort it out for her. When her agent last spoke to her in Paris, the job was guaranteed as hers. Kate was pleased, as this now finally meant the end of Leon and London.

After, as Kate had spent a few days in Orpington getting herself ready and packed for the autumn, she arranged to meet Jane for a farewell get-together.

'Hi, Jane, it's Kate. What are you doing tomorrow?'

'Nothing.'

'Great. Do you want to meet me at our usual spot at London Bridge station?'

'Okay,' replied Jane.

'Well, I will see you at ten o'clock, okay?'

'Yes, see you, Kate.'

'Bye, Jane.'

Jane was glad to hear Kate was back to her normal self again. She was looking forward to meeting her. It would be like old times.

The next day soon arrived. Kate quickly got up and made her way to the train station. She was really looking forward to seeing Jane and telling her about the trip around Europe and her new job.

As she arrived at London Bridge she found Jane waiting for her outside W H Smiths.

'Hello, Jane.'

'Hello, Kate. You look wonderful.'

'Thanks, Jane. Well, do you fancy grabbing a coffee somewhere, as I have something important to tell you.'

'Really, Kate? Have you found a nice Italian man and you're getting married to him?'

'Oh no, it's nothing like that.'

Kate and Jane then headed to a quiet tea room alongside the river. It was a nice little place. Kate had been there many times before with Jane, but this time will be the last for a while at least.

'What are you having?' asked the waitress politely.

'Oh, two cappuccinos please,' replied Kate.

'Okay, coming right up,' said the waitress.

'Well, Kate, what exciting news do you have?'

'Well, Jane,' replied Kate rather slowly. 'I've got a new job, actually it's more like a fresh start.'

'Tell me more.'

'I've exhausted London and I don't really feel safe any more with Leon living down here. So I have a new job as composer in residence based at Edinburgh University.'

'Oh I see, Kate,' said Jane, disappointedly.

'Well, don't look disappointed, Jane – I am not emigrating to Australia or anything. I still have two more weeks before moving to Scotland. I need to get away, Jane, somewhere where Leon cannot hurt me and I know in Scotland he cannot do that. Even his friends. Speaking of which, there is one of them over there.'

'Where?'

'Sitting at the table nearest to the counter. Don't look, he'll only come over and give me a hard time.'

'You don't know that, Kate. Why don't we go over to sit with him. Then you can tell him the truth about his so-called friend Leon. Tell him some lie to pass on like you're getting married to some guy in Switzerland and working in some university out there.'

'All right, why not?' replied Kate eagerly. 'At least then I would have got my revenge before moving up north.'

Kate and Jane proceeded to walk over to where Leon's friend called Craig was sitting.

'Hi, Craig. Do you mind if we join you?' asked Kate.

'Great, it's good to see you both, especially you, Kate. So

where's Leon?'

'He's in bed pissed,' replied Kate vivaciously.

Craig was quite surprised to see Kate with her friend Jane and with no Leon around. He thought that she and Leon were still an item.

Jane led most of the conversation. She told Craig all about Leon and what a pig he was towards Kate. Kate then gloated about her new job in Switzerland and about the new guy she was planning to marry. Craig seemed to have believed her. He was shocked to find out all about what kind of friend Leon really was.

'Well, Kate, I must be going,' said Craig. 'It was good to see you again and good luck in Switzerland.'

'Thanks, Craig. Bye.'

As soon as Craig had left, Jane and Kate burst out laughing. It had been a long time the two girls had laughed together. Kate, now relieved that Leon was finally out of her life and mind, could actually laugh at him. Before she could not have done this.

'Well, Jane, you are welcome to come to Scotland and stay with me. Edinburgh is a great city, you'll love it.'

'I'll see, Kate. Darren and I are getting married next year.'

'Oh great. Well look, I'm going to have to go back to Orpington. I have loads of things to do before I go to Edinburgh.'

'I understand, Kate. I'll walk you to the station.'

'No, Jane. I'll be fine. Besides I thought you would be meeting Darren later.'

'Yes, well. I'll see you soon, Kate.'

'Bye, Jane.'

Kate then left the tea room and walked back to London Bridge station for the 13.33 train to Orpington.

Once at home and in bed, the phone rang. It was two o'clock in the morning.

'Oh God,' cried Kate. 'What does he want?'

Kate decided to answer the phone for the last time. She recorded the conversation, so that in the morning she could get rid of him once and for all by going to the police.

'I should have gone to the police when he assaulted me,' thought Kate. 'That way I wouldn't be suffering now.'

'What do you want?' asked Kate viciously.

'What do I want, you fucking stupid little whore, telling Craig what I did to you. Who the fuck are you, Kate? Kate?'

'Oh I'm here, Leon. What do you mean?'

'Okay, I hit you a little – you didn't have to tell Craig. You've destroyed my life, how could you?'

'Well, Leon, I think you have done that to yourself.'

'No, you fucking bitch, I haven't done anything to myself.'

'Look, Leon, I must go – work calls me tomorrow.'

Kate then hung up on him. Leon tried to phone back several times, but in the end Kate just switched off the phone.

The next day Kate went to the police station to report Leon for making malicious phone calls. The police were very sympathetic and helped her to change her mobile number.

Now, Leon can never get hold of me again, thought Kate with a smile. Two weeks later Kate started to say farewell to her family, and to Jane.

'Time now to get the train to Edinburgh and to start a new life up north,' said Kate excitedly. 'Bye, mum. Bye, dad.'

'Bye, darling,' replied her parents.

Later Kate left Orpington for a new life in Scotland. But as far as Leon is concerned, no one will ever know what happened to him. Kate hoped he would have been thrown out and was living a miserable life.

But for now that is all in the past, and Leon will stay in the past. As far as Kate is concerned, Edinburgh is now her future, and present, and no one is ever going to be allowed to hurt her like that again. Kate will not let it happen. Not for now anyway…